TERS

Song by **Bill Staines**
Pictures by **Kadir Nelson**

SIMON & SCHUSTER BOOKS FOR YOUNG READERS
New York • London • Toronto • Sydney

All God's Critters

got a place in the choir—
Some sing low,
some sing higher,
Some sing out loud
on the telephone wire,
and some just clap
their hands, or paws,
or anything they got. Now . . .

Listen to the bass,
it's the one on the bottom,
where the **bullfrog** croaks
and the **hippopotamus**
moans and groans
with **a** big to-do.

And the old cow just goes,

The **dog** and the **cat** they take up the middle, while the **honeybee** hums and the **cricket** fiddles.

All God's critters got a place in the choir—
Some sing low, some sing higher,
Some sing out loud on the telephone wire,

and some just clap their hands, or paws, or anything they got. Now . . .

Listen to the top where the **little birds** sing
on the melodies with the high notes ringing.
The **hoot owl** hollers over everything,
and the **jaybird** disagrees.

Singin' in the nighttime, singin' in the day,
the **little duck** quacks, then he's on his way.

The **possum** ain't got much to say, and the **porcupine** talks to himself.

All God's Critters
got a place in the choir—
Some sing low,
some sing higher,
some sing out loud
on the
telephone
wire,

and some just clap their hands, or paws, or anything they got. Now . . .

It's a simple song of livin'
sung everywhere,
by the OX and the fox
and the grizzly bear,
the grumpy alligator
and the hawk above,
the sly raccoon
and the turtledove.

All God's Critters got a place in the Choir— some sing low,

some sing
higher,
some sing out
loud on the
telephone wire,

and some just clap their hands,

or paws, or anything they got. Now!

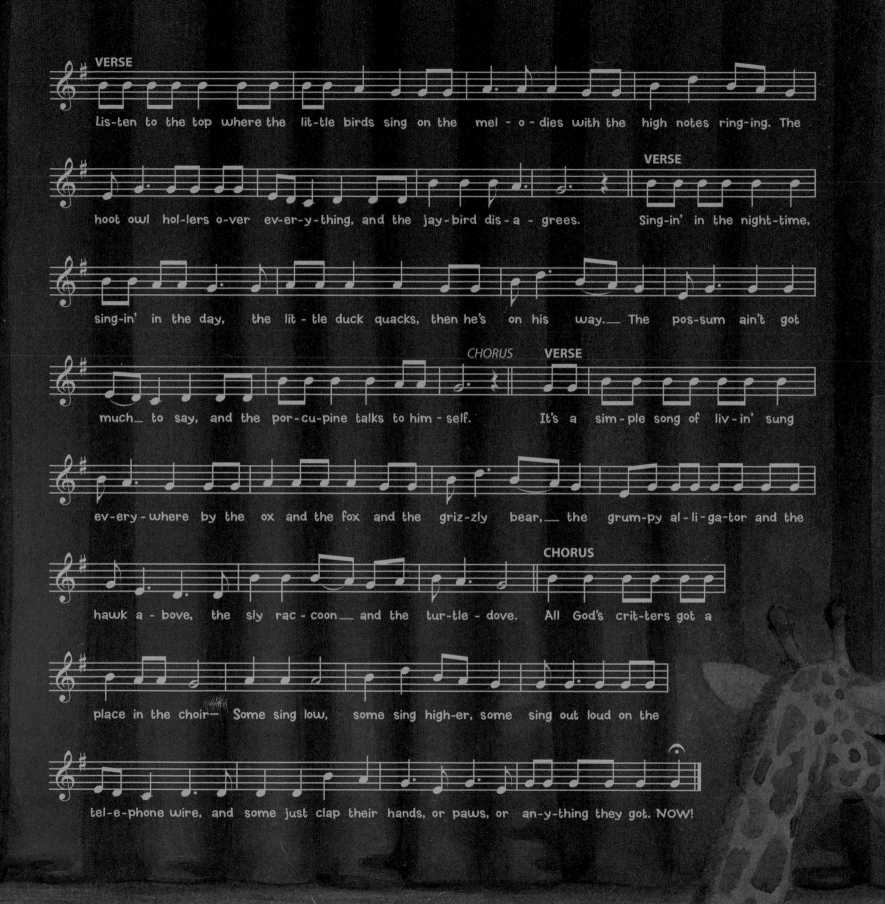

SIMON & SCHUSTER
BOOKS FOR YOUNG READERS
An imprint of Simon & Schuster
Children's Publishing Division
1230 Avenue of the Americas, New York, New York 10020
"All God's Critters Got a Place in the Choir"
written by Bill Staines © 1978
MINERAL RIVER MUSIC (BMI)
ADMINISTERED BY BUG MUSIC.
ALL RIGHTS RESERVED.
USED BY PERMISSION.
Illustrations copyright © 2009
by Kadir Nelson, Inc.